AF382465

Thomas Sutton

A Treatise on the Positive Collodion Process

Thomas Sutton

A Treatise on the Positive Collodion Process

Reprint of the original, first published in 1857.

1st Edition 2023 | ISBN: 978-3-37516-072-2

Salzwasser Verlag is an imprint of Outlook Verlagsgesellschaft mbH.

Verlag (Publisher): Outlook Verlag GmbH, Zeilweg 44, 60439 Frankfurt, Deutschland
Vertretungsberechtigt (Authorized to represent): E. Roepke, Zeilweg 44, 60439 Frankfurt, Deutschland
Druck (Print): Books on Demand GmbH, In de Tarpen 42, 22848 Norderstedt, Deutschland

A TREATISE

ON THE

Positive Collodion Process.

BY THOMAS SUTTON, B.A.,

Editor of "Photographic Notes."
Author of a Treatise on the Calotype Process, &c.

LONDON:
BLAND & LONG, 153, FLEET STREET.
1857.

INTRODUCTION.

THE following pages contain full information on the subject of the Positive Collodion Process. I have described minutely how to make the Collodion, and the various solutions required, together with the mode of taking the picture.

I have also offered some remarks on Photographic Portraiture which I trust may be found useful to those who are desirous of producing artistic pictures. I have always endeavoured to give my reasons for what I advance, and to express myself so clearly as to be intelligible to the Tyro in the Art, and nothing has, I believe, been omitted that can contribute to his perfect success in following my directions.

I have observed the great increase during the past year of the number of professional and amateur photographers who practise the Positive Collodion Process exclusively, on account of its economy and adaptation to the requirements of portraiture; but at the same time I have remarked the almost universal bad tone of the pictures exhibited. Now I find that by using proper materials, and observing common precautions, very excellent WHITES, and every other quality of a fine proof, may be obtained;—that it is in fact just as easy to produce a fine white as a dull sombre grey or brown hue in the lights, while this superiority of tone seems all that is required to raise the Glass Positive to the rank of an artistic production. Should the reader therefore be dissatisfied with his present results and anxious to improve them, he will find in the following pages the means of so modifying his formulæ as to produce with equal ease the finest pictures that the process is capable of yielding.

It is therefore because I conceive that I have something new and good to offer that I publish this pamphlet; and in order that I may make it as useful and scientific as possible I make no mystery of any of the details.

Now, having taken great pains in describing the process familiarly and clearly, so that all may understand me, and being sincerely desirous that everyone may succeed with my formulæ, and that a most useful and delightful art may be advanced a step in public estimation, I have a right to require of the reader in return, that he withhold his opinion of my process until he shall have given it a careful and honest trial, following my directions implicitly in all points, great and small.

As example may add weight to precept, I am prepared to send a specimen, by post, to anyone who will apply for it, on the terms stated in the advertisement at the end. A stock of these specimens will always be kept in readiness, and no delay will therefore occur in their transmission. They are portraits, taken from the life by the process described, and with my Collodion. I forward them as specimens of colour : that is, of whites, blacks, and middle tints.

Although I have given the formula for the Collodion, in order that there may be no mystery in the matter, yet I would dissuade the reader from attempting to make it himself. It is a troublesome and delicate job, involving a knowledge of chemical manipulation, and requiring purer chemicals than can be ordinarily obtained from the chemist. Foggy, feeble, and spotty pictures are the inevitable result of using common chemicals, even when their purity is believed in and guaranteed by the vendor. I have arranged to manufacture the Collodion on a large scale, with materials properly purified and tested, and those who employ my formulæ will do well to obtain the collodion of me. The great secret of a good collodion consists, not in the addition to it of any empirical foreign substance, but in the purity and proper strength of the ordinary materials with which it is made, and the careful superintendence of the manufacture. This careful superintendence I guarantee; and I shall introduce any real improvement which may at any time be discovered.

On the subject of Colouring Positives I have been somewhat brief, for the fact is, I much prefer a good photograph uncoloured; and although an amateur artist, and formerly a pupil of Sass, of Bloomsbury, I have rarely tried my hand at tinting photographs. However, with the kind help of a friend who has had much experience in this matter, I have ventured to offer some remarks on Colouring.

I shall always be happy to reply to the queries of correspondents through the medium of my fortnightly Journal, "*Photographic Notes.*"

I think I may say with confidence that the Positive Collodion process, as described in these pages, is at once the simplest and cheapest of all Photographic processes. The pictures produced by it appear to be quite permanent, when protected from the influence of a sulphuretted atmosphere.

THOMAS SUTTON.

St. Brelade's Bay, Jersey,
    March 10*th*, 1857.

CHAPTER I.

ON PHOTOGRAPHIC PORTRAITURE.

LIGHT AND SHADE; POSE AND EXPRESSION; ACCESSORIES OF A PHOTOGRAPHIC PORTRAIT; AND ARTISTIC CONSIDERATIONS GENERALLY.

Photographic portraiture is not a mere mechanical art. A good photographic portrait is something more than a successful piece of manipulation. It involves the application of certain principles of art, the knowledge of which is essential to success. The mere photographer, in ignorance of these principles, may produce a copy of the human face, considered as a material body exposed to light, but he will never, except by a lucky chance, produce a pleasing portrait of his sitter. I cannot therefore do better than commence this treatise with a discussion of those essential points which determine the character of a portrait as an artistic production, viz., the pose, the effect of light and shade, and the arrangement of the background and accessories. The reader who prefers proceeding at once to the details of the manipulation of the process can do so, and return to the present chapter; but the natural order of things requires that its contents should precede the rest.

I begin then with some considerations on the subject of Light and Shade.

ON LIGHT AND SHADE.

In treating of light and shade, I shall show first that in nature these lie between much wider limits than can be assigned to them in artistic representations, at the same time that there is in nature a perfectly graduated scale of shade between the highest light and the deepest shadow, without any gap. From this I conclude that in works of art, where the limits of black and white are assigned, there should be between those limits a graduated scale corresponding exactly with that in nature. This having been established, I hope to the satisfaction of the reader, (and let him not take it for granted too readily, for the principle is opposed to the practice of some eminent artists) I shall proceed to deduce some general rules which should guide him in the management of the light in photographic portraiture. And let him not think my speculations unpractical, for they lie in fact at the very foundation of Art. My remarks will occupy but a small space, and I commend them to his notice as the result of much careful study.

If we go on a sunny day at noon into any natural scene, and first turn our eyes to the South where the sun is shining, we encounter a flood of light on which it is impossible to keep the eye steadily fixed for an instant. Next, still regarding the sky, if we gradually turn towards the North, we observe the light continually decreasing, until the blue of the northern firmament appears dark compared with the effulgence behind us. If it were possible to cut a square patch out of the northern sky and place it on the southern side of the heavens, it would appear decidedly dark by the contrast. Next, comparing the light of terrestrial objects with that of the sky, we see that those which have a light local colour, and are in full sunshine, appear to be lighter than the blue northern sky, as light perhaps as white clouds ; while those of a dark local colour, such as green foliage, or red tiles, or brown ploughed fields, although in full sunshine, are decidedly darker than the sky. On turning to the objects in shadow we observe that the intensity of their darkness depends, first, on the local tint of the object, and secondly, on the amount of open space in front of it, which permits of its being more or less illuminated by *diffused* light, that is, light reflected from other objects and present in the atmosphere ; so that a white building or chalk cliff in shadow, but illuminated by a strong diffused light from a wide open space in front of it, may appear as light as a ploughed field in full sunshine, or as a slated roof in a *glancing* sunlight ; while the crevices of rocks, or the interstices between the branches and leaves of trees, where no appreciable amount of light, either direct or diffused, enters, constitute absolute blackness. Other circumstances which determine the comparative brightness of an object being—the obliquity of the incidence of the solar rays upon it, and the amount of aqueous vapour and blue air intervening between it and the eye; (distant objects having from this cause a light veil as it were thrown over them, which renders them pale and indistinct.)

Such are the relative intensities of light and shade of objects in a sunny landscape; and it will be seen that the transition from the highest light to the deepest blackness consists of *gradual* steps, not one of which is necessarily wanting. We pass from the glowing orb of the sun, the source of light, to the dazzling portion of the sky which immediately surrounds it, and thence by degrees to the deep blue of the opposite heavens, or the pale distances seen through a veil of misty light;—the blue firmament being darker than the white cottage or chalk cliff in sunshine, and the terrestrial objects decreasing in brightness as they receive the light obliquely, or diffused; until we find ourselves at length prying into the black fissures of rocks, or the black interstices of dense foliage, where no light enters; the sun being the highest light, and these crevices absolute blackness; between which extremes, are found every intermediate shade. When the sun is obscured by clouds, everything is seen by diffused light, which is less in intensity than when the sun is shining; and all the bright sunny patches which then contrast so violently with the shadows are now wanting; so that in this case we commence at a lower step in the scale than before.

The extremes of light and shade, although connected by perfect gradations, are therefore in nature very widely separated. So violent in fact are the extreme contrasts, that the eye can only encounter and estimate them by means of the power it possesses of contracting and dilating the pupil.

Let us now turn to Art, and inquire how Art, under these circumstances, can fairly represent Nature. White paper is the whitest substance we can employ for a picture, which is to be viewed by the diffused light that enters through the window of an ordinary apartment. How then can we, on a piece of white paper, lighted by so feeble a diffused light, represent the glorious brightness of the external world, some of the shadows of which may be even lighter than our highest lights, while our deepest shadows are not crevices in which no light can enter, but black marks exposed to diffused light?

The very foundation of Art lies in the reply to this question; and it appears to me to have but one solution. Conceive the range between the highest light and deepest shadow of the natural objects to be represented, as divided into a certain number of gradations; and conceive the range between white and black paper, as divided into the *same* number of shades. Then consider to what gradation of the natural scale the shade of any natural object belongs, and represent it in the picture by the same gradation of the artificial scale. In this way every object in the picture will receive its true *relative* shade, and the result will be that the mind will receive a *truthful suggestion*. We require no more than this in Art, for the imagination does the rest.

And now for the practical application of the above, shall I say, truism to the purposes of Photographic Portraiture.

A Positive Photograph is about to be taken on glass. The most intense black is the black varnish seen through the clear glass in the diffused light of a common apartment; and the highest light is metallic silver, in a state a few shades less white than white paper. The blacks of a glass positive are therefore blacker than those of an engraving, while the lights are not so white. On the whole the range is perhaps about the same in both cases.

We have next to consider the powers of Photography; which it appears are limited. The sensitive plate must be exposed for a certain time to the image of the object formed on it in the camera, the lights and shadows being exposed together. But the light parts receive enough exposure before the shadows, and after that a reverse action takes place in them. It is not true in Photography that the longer the exposure the whiter the lights become, for after the proper exposure has been given to them they deteriorate and become solarized, that is, darker and of bad colour. Here then is a difficulty which must be met by skilful management.

Now then, for the application of our principles. In order to meet the requirements of the problem, it is evident that what I have called the natural scale must, in portraiture, be made to lie within narrow limits. In out-of-door

Photography we must take the light as we find it. The natural scale of light and shade is determined, and we cannot modify it. But in portraiture the case is different. Here we are at liberty to modify the amount, and alter the direction of the light at pleasure; and in so doing it is obvious that, in order to avoid a photographic difficulty, we must reduce the natural scale to certain narrow limits. In other words, the contrasts of light and shade on the face and dress of the sitter must not be too violent; for this would introduce a photographic difficulty *without yielding bolder contrasts in the picture.* This conclusion follows inevitably from what I have said, and I have endeavoured to impress it on the mind of the reader, as a practical truth with which he is much concerned. I repeat then, that a picture, as bold in the contrasts as it is possible to obtain, may be produced without introducing such strong contrasts of light and shade on the model as are generally deemed necessary.

The practical conclusions at which I arrive are,—that a strong light is objectionable in portraiture, because the powers of photography to give good whites are sufficiently taxed when the sitter is placed in a subdued light. The attempt to overstrain these powers defeats its object by destroying the middle tints.

A great fault in many positive portraits appears to me to be, that the face has been sacrificed to the dress. A less amount of light or a shorter exposure would have sufficed, had the dress been of a lighter colour, or had the light been better directed. But the artist feels called on to bring out honestly, and by dint of exposure, the full details of the darkest costume, however badly lighted; and thus the finer shades of the lights are buried, and the face loses its roundness and beauty of half-tone.

Nothing is so easy to copy by photography as an engraving, because the natural scale of shade is then the same as that of the photograph. But in taking a portrait from nature, the natural scale is widened. The range between the highest light and deepest shadow is not then, as in an engraving, that between white, and *black in full light*, but that between white (a white cravat suppose), and *black in shadow* (the creases of a black dress).

The sitter should be placed in a north, or north-east light, which should enter the room from above at an angle of 45° Be careful to avoid a horizontal source of light. This destroys the shadows under the brows, the nose, the lower lip, and the chin, and gives the face a flat appearance. Avoid also a vertical light, which makes the hair on the top of the head look snowy. Shadows are necessary to give the appearance of solidity and rotundity to objects, but they are destroyed by introducing more than one source of light, or by using a too diffused light. There should be one predominant source of light from above, falling obliquely on the sitter.

This oblique light should be directed more to one side of the face than the other, in order that one side may be slightly darker than the other. If the reader will buy a small bust of Napoleon, and throw the light of a candle on it in the manner which I have described, he will find the best possible effect produced, and the experiment will be a valuable one.

Having thus arranged the source of light, white screens should be introduced so as to diminish the blackness of the shadows and the too great force of the contrasts. One of these screens should be brought near the dark side of the sitter. The others are to be used as occasion may require. The floor of the portrait room should be covered with light oilcloth, in order to throw a faint reflected light upwards. The end of the apartment opposite to the sitter should be blackened, in order to avoid a front horizontal light, and for another reason to be stated presently.

A good artist is well aware of the value of reflex lights. He knows that without reflex light a shadow becomes a dark uniform patch, but with it a space full of variety and beauty. There is nothing more charming than to notice in a fine work of art the observance of the laws of reflex lights. Where the main light strikes a rounded object at a tangent there is a deep line of shade, and beyond that, in the shadow, a play of reflex light, depending in amount on the local colour of the objects from which light is reflected, and increasing in brightness as the part in shadow recedes from the tangential line of deepest shade. The reader will easily understand this by an experiment or two, and when he has appreciated my meaning, and observed the value of the reflex lights, he will understand the use of the white screens, and employ them to great advantage.

It has been said of the works of certain eminent painters, that they are perfectly stereoscopic. These fine effects are realised simply by a careful study of the laws of perspective, and light and shade. No single picture can be stereoscopic; but the remark shows the importance of attending to these matters,

Glass is of no other use than to protect the sitter from the wind and weather. In all other respects it is better away. It increases the time of exposure by 30 per cent.

I think I have now sufficiently discussed the question of light and shade. The next points to consider are Pose and Expression.

POSE AND EXPRESSION.

It has been said that Photography does not copy successfully the human face ; that it exaggerates the width of the mouth and chin, diminishes the forehead, magnifies every wrinkle and defect, makes the eye look that of a dead fish, and gives a fixed and painful expression to the features ;— that, in short, photographic portraits are hideous caricatures.

All this, and more than this, may be true of *bad* photographic portraits, but the evils complained of may be avoided, and are to be traced, not to the truthful and marvellous process which *fixes* the image of the camera obscura, but to the image itself. In proof of this, let any one watch the ordinary process of taking a bad photographic portrait. Observe how miserable the sitter looks during the few seconds of the exposure, with the features rigidly set, and the eyes nearly put out by staring at the light ; and contrast this with the expression of relief that comes over the face the instant the sitting is over. Before complaining that photography is in fault, let us endeavour first to obtain a presentable image on the ground glass, and we may then rest perfectly sure that photography will copy it faithfully.

The question of pose and expression resolves itself into this :—the sitter must remain for a few seconds in an easy natural position, with an agreeable expression of countenance. The photographer requires no more than this. His art cannot idealize, or flatter ; it can merely represent a thing as it appears at the time ; he must not therefore aspire to rival the artist. The moment he attempts to rise into the regions of art by employing artifices to take common things out of their own sphere, his work becomes ridiculous, for his artifices are always detected. A photographic portrait is not therefore to be criticised according to the same principles as a work of art, but to be considered as a faithful record of a fact, which should be presented under its most agreeable aspect.

It is considered a pleasant event to visit a photographic studio and have one's portrait taken. There is no reason therefore why any one should look unusually severe and disagreeable when placed opposite to a photographic camera. People do not usually begin to scowl the moment they are condemned to sit for a few seconds in one position. The reason why photographic portraits have so frequently an unpleasant expression is not therefore quite obvious, but I think I can explain it. I have now been looking at the word "position" for ten seconds without experiencing the least disposition to look graver than usual. I could have had my portrait taken twice over in that time. But the word "position" is written on white paper. If I turn my back to the light and look at an ink bottle standing on a shelf in a dark corner of the room, I find that I can keep my eye on it, (not staring at it but thinking of something else and counting) for full twenty seconds without the slightest inconvenience. But if I look out of window at a particular bright spot in the sky, I have no sooner counted five than a film seems to come over my eyes, and I have no doubt I begin to look grave and severe. I conclude, therefore, that too much light entering the eye produces an unpleasant sensation, and consequently an unpleasant expression.

I believe, therefore, that the cause of the unpleasant expression frequently observed in Photographic portraits is simply this,—that the eyes of the sitter have been made to blink and stare at too strong a light. The pupils then involuntarily contract; the eyelids are drawn together; the brows pucker up at the corners next the nose, and an expression of discomfort pervades every feature of the face. But this not only induces an unpleasant expression: it causes that dead fishy appearance of the eyes to which I have alluded. The cornea of the eye is a horny polished surface, which reflects light; consequently the glare of light immediately opposite to the eye strikes the cornea perpendicularly, and is reflected straight into the camera. The eye therefore looks white and fishy, instead of dark and liquid. In order to obtain a large pupil and a dark eye, the eye should be directed into absolute darkness, such as a dark passage, or cellar, and the perfect comfort of this arrangement will ensure, if anything can do so, a fine dark eye and a happy expression.

The principal source of light on the sitter should (as I have said before) fall obliquely from above; and in front of him there should be, either absolute darkness, or a black cloth in shadow hung behind the camera. The perfect comfort of this arrangement ought to ensure a pleasing expression. A light oilcloth on the floor serves to diffuse an upward light, and relieve the shadows under the brows.

POSE.

It is impossible to lay down any rules on this subject, but one thing is certain,—the sitter should not appear to be sitting for his portrait. Whatever he is made to do, whether merely to sit and think, or to be engaged in some occupation, as reading, writing, &c., he should be caught unconscious that his portrait is being taken. The posture, whether sitting or standing, should be natural and easy, and the sitter should not appear to be acting a part.

It is questionable in my mind, how far Photography may be legitimately applied to purposes of picture-making. The artifices employed are generally too obvious. We may admire the cleverness of the attempt, and yet be unable to help smiling at it. Composition is, I think, a province into which Photography should not intrude; but simple portraiture is one of the most useful and legitimate applications of it.

There should be no conceit or affectation in dress. The ordinary everyday costume always looks the best. When there is any option in the matter, the dress should not be black, or very dark, as that introduces a photographic difficulty for which the face has to pay the penalty. Blues come out lighter, and yellows and greens darker than they really appear. Whatever colour the dress may be, there will always be sufficiently rich shadows in the creases of it.

Portraits are either full length, three-quarter length, half length, or bust. I prefer the mere head and shoulders, large, in a circular frame; or shaded off all round, and stuck boldly on the mount. But this' latter plan is only applicable to paper portraits.

ACCESSORIES.

The background should, as a general rule, be dark, not light. Nothing is so odious as a black figure cut sharply on a light background. The colour is not a matter of much importance to a shade or two. It may be made by mixing black, white, red, and yellow. A large sheet painted in distemper, and *graduated*, so as to be darker at the bottom and lighter towards one top corner, forms the best background. It should not, on any account, be varnished, and the dabs of the brush need not be softened off too much.

Backgrounds painted with bits of curtain, balustrade, peeps of distant scenery, &c., are not much to my taste. There may be a prettiness about them, but they are such an obvious sham that they should, I think, be avoided.

The background should be stretched upon a deal frame, with wedges at the corners, like the frame of an oil painting. It should be stretched as flat as possible, and made of one piece of canvass, without a seam, at least 8ft. square.

A chaste simplicity should be observed in the accessories of the portrait, and nothing should be introduced which has a varnished surface.

Common chairs, tables, &c., are rarely artistic. These should be of faultless design, and not French-polished, or the high lights will look like spots of snow.

There must be no appearance of poverty in the accessories of the picture, and as a general rule common things should be avoided, simply because the design of most common things is bad.

I have now exhausted my catalogue of practical hints on the subject of light and shade, pose, expression, and accessories.

CHAPTER II.

ON THE CHEMICALS USED IN THE PROCESS, AND THEIR MODE OF PREPARATION.

OUTLINE OF THE PROCESS.

Pursuing what appears to me to be the natural mode of treating the subject, I shall first give a brief sketch of the process, and then treat more fully of the various chemical substances employed; deferring to another chapter the minute details of the manipulation.

The Positive Collodion Process on Glass is conducted as follows :—

A plate of glass is first cleaned and polished.

Iodized Collodion is then poured upon it.

It is next plunged into a bath, called the Nitrate Bath, which renders it sensitive to light.

It is then exposed to the luminous image formed by the lens in the camera obscura.

The invisible picture then formed on the sensitive plate is developed by pouring on it a solution called the " developer." This brings out the lights of the picture, so that wherever the light has acted the developer throws down a white precipitate ; but produces no precipitate where the light has not acted. There are consequently no shadows to the picture, but merely lights, more or less modulated in tone according to the relative intensity of the light which produced the impression, and the duration of the time of exposure ; so that the picture in this state is formed by lights alone upon a transparent ground.

The picture is then washed with water, and certain redundant chemicals are removed by a process called fixing, which is effected by pouring on the plate a fixing solution. It is then washed again in order to remove all traces of the fixing agent, and dried.

The picture is then varnished with transparent varnish, which protects it from injury ; and on the back of it is poured a dark opaque varnish, which, by forming a dark back-ground to the lights, produces the shadows.

The picture is now finished, and it only remains to secure it in a case. It is called a Positive because the lights and shadows are true to Nature.

The operations are therefore as follow :—
    1st. To clean and polish the plate,
    2nd. To coat it with iodized collodion.
    3rd. To render it sensitive to light.

4th. To expose it in the camera.
5th. To develop the picture.
6th. To fix the picture.
7th. To varnish the picture.

These operations involve the use of the following chemicals :—

The cleansing agent.
Iodized collodion.
The nitrate bath.
The developing solution.
The fixing solution.
The transparent and opaque varnishes.

The remainder of this chapter will be devoted to a description of the mode of preparing the above compounds.

THE CLEANSING AGENT.

The glass plate must be chemically clean. In order to make it so, we must first clean it as we would any other piece of glass, and remove all visible dirt, stains, &c., by washing and rubbing. But a piece of glass or crockery may appear clean and yet not be so chemically. A common dinner plate for instance, although looking fastidiously clean on the rack, may not be so chemically, the surface being in all probability slightly greasy, and the pores of the glaze filled with organic matter. Now, the operations which we are about to conduct are very delicate, and the molecular disturbances, or decompositions, of the sensitive film which are effected by the feeble light of the image in the camera are considerably modified by any roughness of surface of the glass, or by the presence of foreign matter—these circumstances determining, under the action of the developer, the precipitation of silver, just as much as if light had acted on the parts where they occur.

The glass plate being therefore only apparently clean, it remains to render it so chemically.

The best agent for this purpose is NITRIC ACID.

Nitric acid is a powerful oxydiser, and it readily decomposes most kinds of organic matter, such as the grease left by finger marks, dirty cloths, &c. At the same time, it is a quick solvent of any of the salts of silver which might remain in the pores of the glass from a former picture taken on it. Also, should a minute trace of nitric acid remain in the glass, in consequence of insufficient washing, it would do little or no harm.

I recommend therefore Commercial Nitric Acid, as the best cleansing agent, in preference to soda, tripoli, or any other substance. The mode of applying it will be given in the next Chapter.

IODIZED COLLODION.

Iodized Collodion is made, by adding to the plain Collodion used in surgery, an alcoholic solution of an alkaline or metallic iodide.

I shall therefore first describe how to make Plain Collodion, and afterwards how to Iodize it.

MANUFACTURE OF COLLODION.

Collodion (a word derived from the Greek " Kollao " to stick) is a glutinous transparent liquid formed by dissolving a substance called pyroxyline in a mixture of ether and alcohol.

Pyroxyline is obtained by acting on cotton wool or unsized paper by a mixture of nitric and sulphuric acids, and it is commonly called " gun-cotton " or " gun-paper," according to the material of which it is made. Both Cotton and Paper are the same in chemical composition. They merely differ in structure, the fibre being in both cases " lignine."

So far as the result is concerned, it does not matter whether we employ cotton wool or unsized paper in the manufacture of Collodion. But I think cotton the most manageable substance. I shall therefore describe the mode of making Collodion from cotton wool.

But in doing so, I am met at once by a difficulty. The real secret of good Collodion is to have a good sample of gun-cotton, and in order to make good gun-cotton it is necessary to act upon cotton wool with acids of definite strength, in definite proportion, at a definite temperature. Now acids of definite strength are not easily to be obtained. I cannot therefore give an exact formula unless I know the particular strength of the acids to be used. Nor can I construct a table of proportions corresponding exactly with the specific gravities of the acids, because the impurities which the acids may contain affect their specific gravity. I think it better therefore to describe a few experiments, from which the reader will learn more than if I attempted to give him an exact formula.

Procure some dry cotton wool chemically clean, some pure sulphuric acid, S. G. 1.84, some pure nitric acid, S. G. 1.5, and some rectified sulphuric ether, S. G. .750. (*)

Use the fire-place of an out-building for the experiments. Put an old frying pan filled with sand on the fire, and in this sand-bath place a pie-dish containing water heated to about 170° Faht.   Then procure a breakfast cup and a couple of long thick glass rods.

1st Experiment.—Put into the cup

  5 drachms Nitric Acid, by measure.
  5 drachms Sulphuric Acid.
  25 grains Cotton Wool.

(*) The specific gravity of a fluid is the ratio which the weight of a certain volume of it at 60° Faht., bears to the weight of an equal volume of distilled water at the same temperature   The ratio being expressed by a decimal fraction.

The best way of testing the specific gravity of fluids is by means of a specific gravity bottle. This bottle when filled with distilled water at 60° Faht. contains exactly 1000 grains. To test the specific gravity of any fluid, we have therefore to fill the bottle with the fluid at a temperature of 60° Faht, and weigh it in a good pair of scales. If we first balance the empty bottle by a piece of lead, the remaining weight estimated in grains and considered as the numerator of a fraction, the denominator of which is 1000, will be the specific gravity of the fluid. The bottle must be wiped perfectly dry before putting it into the scales.

Tested in this way, a specific gravity bottle full of the sulphuric acid with which we are about to operate, would weigh the piece of lead which balances the empty bottle, plus 1840 grains; this divided by 1000 gives 1.840 the S. G. required.

Dense suffocating fumes rise from the mixture ; these should escape up the chimney. Keep working the cotton wool about with the glass rods for 5 minutes, during which time the temperature of the mixture should be 140°. The temperature of the water in which the cup stands being about 170°, that of the mixture in the cup will be as nearly as possible 140° ; but you must test it with a thermometer, the ball of which can be inserted in the mixture ; for the preservation of an even temperature is of the utmost importance.

At the end of five minutes, remove the cup, throw away the mixed acids, and put the cotton into a pail of water. Wash it quickly, opening it well, and rousing it about in the water. Then continue the washing in a basin, changing the water several times, and squeezing the cotton after each washing between your hands.

When you have thoroughly washed and squeezed out all traces of the acids in this way, pull the cotton out into a large loose ball, and hang it up to dry gradually in a clean piece of netting. The cotton when dry looks pretty much as it did at first, but you feel a peculiar harshness about it.

The first experiment yields Pyroxyline of the most explosive kind. Be careful therefore of accidents.

Repeat the experiment ten or twelve times, adding in the second experiment 30 minims of water to the acids, and increasing the quantity of water added by 30 minims in each fresh experiment. The twelfth experiment will therefore contain, in addition to the acids, 330 minims, i.e. $5\frac{1}{2}$ drachms of water.

I will now suppose the various samples of gun-cotton to be dry, and ready for an investigation of their properties.

First—weigh them.

<pre>
        Sample 1 will weigh 43 grains.
           „   2   „   43   „
           „   3   „   43   „
           „   4   „   42   „
           „   5   „   37   „
        Samples 6, 7, 8 „   37   „
</pre>

The cotton having increased in weight from 75 to 50 per cent., according to the quantity of water added.

We now proceed to test the solubility of these twelve samples of gun cotton in Ether, S.G. .750, and also to ascertain the various properties of the film produced when the solution is poured on a glass plate. I may observe that Ether, at .750, contains a proportion of alcohol and water ; the S.G. of absolute Ether, being only .720.

Weigh two grains of each sample of gun cotton, and test their respective solubility in half an ounce of Ether. Samples 1, 2, and 3, will be found to be insoluble. Sample 4 looks more gelatinous, and seems inclined to dissolve. Sample 5 dissolves completely on shaking the bottle. Samples 6, 7, 8, 9, 10, are soluble ; 11 partly so ; 12 not at all.

Now compare the different samples of cotton. The first three or four are long and fibrous, the next three or four get somewhat shorter, the last three or four become very short, and break up into little short shreds, many of which are lost in the washing.

The first three or four samples are called " Pyroxyline," and the last three or four " Xyloidine."   But it will be seen that this nomenclature is imperfect, for it does not include the middle varieties, which are those with which we are concerned in Photography, viz :—Nos. 5, 6, 7 and 8.   I will call them Photographic gun-cotton.

The first samples of Pyroxyline are highly explosive. Place a small tuft on the hearth, and apply to it the end of a red hot piece of iron wire.   It instantly goes off " puff," without smoke, and leaving no ash.   The last varieties of Xyloidine are merely combustible, and not explosive.

Let us next examine the nature of the solutions made with samples between Nos. 5 and 10.

Pour a few drops of No. 5 on the finger, so that it may run round both ways. It dries quickly (producing a sensation of cold), and, when dry, contracts strongly, looking like a piece of goldbeater's skin, stuck tightly round the finger. This is the hard contractile collodion.   Its use should be avoided in Photography.

Now pour a few drops of No. 10 on the finger.   This also dries quickly, but when dry does not contract like the former, and instead of being transparent, is semi-opaque, or " opalescent," or " papyraceous," looking like a piece of tissue paper stuck round the finger.   This is also a kind of Collodion to be avoided in Photography.

The proper variety of gun - cotton for Photographic purposes lies between these extremes.

In order to try which is the best, pour a little of each solution on a clean glass plate.   But in order to make the experiment fairly, wait a day or two, until the floating particles in the collodion have settled to the bottom of the bottle ; for you cannot properly filter collodion.

Examine the films before a strong light, with the help of a magnifier.

Film No. 5 is not only hard and contractile, but shows structure, being covered with wavy marks, or lines.

Films No. 6 and 7 are much better and are nearly structureless ; No. 6 is the best.

Film No. 8 begins to get slightly opaque.

In films Nos. 9 and 10, the opacity increases.

No. 6 is therefore the best collodion, and on adding a little alcohol to it, the appearance of structure in the film altogether vanishes.   It adheres tightly to the glass, without contracting, and cannot easily be washed off.

The reader will now understand that the manufacture of gun-cotton is a matter of considerable nicety, there being, out of twelve samples made by varying the proportions of water, only one that can be called first-rate.

In the manufacture of gun-cotton, Nitric Acid, S.G. 1.4, will answer the purpose.   I merely used a stronger sample for the purpose of illustration.

Mr. Hardwich recommends rather more sulphuric acid and rather less water than I find to be the best. On these points the reader had better be guided by his own experiments.

It is better to make small quantities of gun-cotton at a time. It always happens in making large quantities that a portion of the cotton remains unacted on by the acids, and this does not, of course, dissolve in the Ether, but remains suspended in it in the state of floating particles. Never purchase gun cotton that is dusty, in consequence of having been carelessly made in too large quantities.

Having now shown how to make the gun-cotton, I will give the formula for the Iodized Collodion.

Either the Iodide of Potassium, or Ammonium, or Cadmium may be employed ; but I prefer the Iodide of Ammonium. It certainly gives cleaner and more vigorous pictures than Iodide of Cadmium, and the film is free from the little transparent spots which generally occur when Iodide of Potassium is used, and which are no doubt due, as Mr. Charles Long affirms, to undissolved crystals of Iodide of Potassium; this salt being much less soluble in Alcohol than Iodide of Ammonium. The instability of Iodide of Ammonium is of no consequence in Positive Collodion, because the presence of a little free Iodine is an advantage rather than not. In Negative Collodion the case is somewhat different. The principal objection to Iodide of Cadmium is, that the Iodide of Silver formed from it, is very sensitive to heat.

The use of bromides, chlorides, &c., appears to be unnecessary.

The formula for Iodized Collodion is therefore as follows :—

IODIZED COLLODION.

Add six parts Rectified Sulphuric Ether, S. G. .750 to two parts pure Alcohol, S. G. .820.

Every ounce of this mixture must contain 4 grains of gun-cotton, and 4 grains of pure Iodide of Ammonium.

In making the compound, first dissolve in the Ether the whole of the gun-cotton; then dissolve the whole of the Iodide of Ammonium in the Alcohol. Mix the solutions if you intend to use them shortly, or keep them separate if not wanted within two or three months.

The plain Collodion improves by keeping, if you keep the bottle in a cool place, quite full, and well stoppered. Never shake it, but allow all floating particles to settle to the bottom. The gun cotton is decomposed gradually, and flat crystals are precipitated.

The iodizing solution does not keep so well. It becomes discolored, from the liberation of free iodine, but it may be used in this state apparently without any disadvantage.

The iodized collodion must not be used when first iodized. Wait at least a week before using it. It appears to improve by keeping, up to about six weeks or a couple of months, and may even be used successfully for certain purposes when of a dark sherry colour.

This collodion may also be used for negatives, but it does not give quite the same density as when Iodide of Potsssium is employed. The latter salt is the best for negative collodion, and is that which I find, on analysis, Mr. Thomas uses in his Xylo-Iodide of Silver. This compound may be matched exactly by substituting pure Iodide of Potassium for Iodide of Ammonium in the above iodizing solution. My plain collodion is the same apparently as Mr. Thomas's.

A few words now on the THEORY OF PYROXYLINE.

Pyroxyline is produced by acting on Lignin with Nitro-Sulphuric Acid. Lignin is composed of Carbon, Oxygen, and Hydrogen; and chemically clean cotton wool is nearly a pure specimen of it.

On the addition of Nitro-Sulphuric acid, an atom of the Oxygen of the Nitric Acid takes an atom of the Hydrogen of the Lignin and forms water, and the Peroxide of Nitrogen, into which the Nitric Acid has been converted by the loss of an atom of Oxygen, steps into the place of the Hydrogen and forms the *substitution compound* Pyroxyline. In this reaction the part played by the Sulphuric acid has been stated to be, that in consequence of its affinity for water, it prevents the Pyroxyline from being dissolved in the remainder of the Nitric Acid, for it appears that Pyroxyline is soluble in dilute though not in strong Nitric Acid.

Sufficient has now been said on the subject of the manufacture of the collodion.

THE NITRATE BATH.

This is made as follows :—

1 ounce distilled water,
40 grains Nitrate of Silver,
1 minim pure Nitric Acid, S. G. 1. 4.

In order to add a small quantity of Iodide of Silver to the bath, coat a plate with iodised collodion, immerse it in the bath, and leave it in all night.   The next morning the yellow Iodide of Silver at first formed in the film will most probably be found dissolved in the bath.

Nitrate of Silver is sometimes adulterated with Nitrate of Soda, or Nitrate of Potass.   The following means of testing the actual amount of Nitrate of Silver contained in a drachm of the bath, will be found useful :—

Take pure crystallised Chloride of Sodium, and dry it perfectly.   Then dissolve 8½ grains in 6 fluid ounces of distilled water.   A drachm of this solution will decompose exactly half-a-grain of Nitrate of Silver, when added to a Nitrate Bath, and will precipitate white insoluble Chloride of Silver.

Take therefore a measured drachm of the Nitrate Bath to be tested, and add to it small quantities of the above solution of salt, until no more Chloride of Silver can be precipitated. Then, the quantity of solution of salt employed is a test of the quantity of Nitrate of Silver present in a drachm of the nitrate bath.

If the Nitrate of Silver is pure, it would require 10 drachms of salt solution to throw down the whole of the silver in a drachm of the bath.

THE DEVELOPING SOLUTION.

Dissolve 1 ounce of powdered Nitrate of Baryta in 16 ounces of water, and when dissolved add 2 drachms of Nitric Acid, S.G., 1.4. Next add 1½ ounces of powdered Proto-Sulphate of Iron. Shake well until the iron salt is dissolved. The mixture becomes white and turbid, in consequence of the formation of Sulphate of Baryta. Let it stand a few hours, until this has settled to the bottom of the vessel; then decant and filter the solution, which, if right, will be of an apple-green colour. Add 2 ounces of Alcohol, to enable it to flow freely over the Collodion film. This is the Developing Solution.

An ounce of Proto-Sulphate of Iron decomposes about an ounce of Nitrate of Baryta, forming insoluble Sulphate of Baryta, and soluble Proto-Nitrate of Iron. The remaining half-ounce of undecomposed Proto-Sulphate of Iron forms the energetic part of the developer.

The Nitric Acid should be added as stated, and not *after* the iron salt, as some peroxidation of the iron might then occur, which would occasion a browning of the solution, and would be injurious.

If kept in a cool place the developer will remain good for several weeks. As it gradually becomes weaker by keeping, its toning properties sometimes improve; when too weak it may be strengthened and rendered tolerably good by the addition of more Proto-Sulphate of Iron.

The developer contains, therefore, two parts of Proto-Nitrate of Iron to one part of Proto-Sulphate of Iron; together with a certain proportion of Nitric Acid and Alcohol.

By using the above Bath and Developer with a full-bodied Collodion, properly made and iodized, magnificent whites may be produced, as well as beautiful gradations of middle tint. It will be seen that I have abandoned altogether the use of Acetic Acid in this process.

My reasons for recommending the above formula will be given in a future chapter, when treating of the theory of this process. I shall then show that the beauty of the whites, and the preservation of the half-tones, depend much on the developer employed.

THE FIXING SOLUTION.

I am obliged to recommend the use of Cyanide of Potassium as a fixing agent in preference to Hypo-Sulphite of Soda (which may be used for fixing negatives), because the cyanide certainly gives a better tone to the picture. It appears that whenever Hypo-Sulphite of Soda is used as a means of removing the redundant chemicals, that a small amount of sulphuration of the silver in the image unavoidably occurs; and in the case of Positives on Glass, it is no doubt this circumstance which injures more or less the brilliancy of the whites. Cyanide of Potassium must therefore be employed. In using it, the reader must remember that it is one of the most deadly poisons known. A small quantity, even, of dilute solution of this substance getting into any scratch, or cut on the fingers, irritates and inflames the part, and has been known to cause considerable swelling of the hand and arm. It will be therefore a good plan to avoid the risk, by pouring a few drops of *plain* collodion over any cuts or scratches on the hands. This, on drying, will form a tight and impervious film over the part, and so protect it from the action of the cyanide.

The proportions of the fixing solution are as follow, but much latitude is allowable :—

> 1 ounce water,
> 5 grains Cyanide of Potassium.

TRANSPARENT VARNISH.

This varnish is used in order to protect the picture from injury, and from atmospheric influences. It is made thus :—
Dissolve half-an-ounce (or thereabouts) of Gum Dammar, powdered very fine, in ten ounces of Benzole. Pure Benzole is the best, because the varnish is then as colourless as water; but common Benzole is much cheaper.

This varnish may be used either for Positives or Negatives. It dries quickly, and does not require the plate to be heated.

BLACK VARNISH.

This varnish, when poured on the back of the plate, forms a black background to the picture. It is made thus :—

First, add together four ounces of powdered Asphaltum, and one ounce of common Benzole. Mix intimately.

Next, dissolve one ounce of India rubber in two ounces of Benzole.

Add the mixtures together. They form a good black varnish, which, I believe, will not crack if the plate is kept in a dry place. Damp is the principal cause of the cracking of varnish.

The chemicals required in this process are therefore as follow :—

Nitric Acid.	Nitrate of Baryta.
Iodized Collodion.	Proto-Sulphate of Iron.
Nitrate of Silver.	Cyanide of Potassium.
Alcohol.	Transparent Varnish.

Black Varnish.

CHAPTER III.

The room in which the plate is sensitized, and the picture developed, has been called the " Operating Room " or " Dark Room." The latter term is the shortest and perhaps the best.

This room should be covered with oilcloth, if it is thought necessary to save the floor from stains. It should have a small north window ; or if that aspect is not practicable, the window should have a shutter outside, opening with hinges at the top, so as to shade it from the sun. The window should have a wooden sliding panel at the bottom, capable of being pushed easily backwards and forwards within two rebates. The rest of the window should be covered, first with two layers of white calico, then with three layers of yellow calico. The object of the sliding panel is to let in white light quickly when the picture is being fixed.

A bench should be placed immediately under the window ; and on this should stand a wooden sink, having a shelf across it at one end, and at the other end a hole and spout to carry off the waste water into a pail beneath, or into a drain. Over the sink, at the end opposite to the shelf, there should be a tap from which fresh water may be obtained. This tap should be of moderate size. If the water is not laid on, a zinc bucket with a tap at the bottom will answer the purpose. This must be supported at a proper height above the sink, and filled as occasion may require.

The shelf across the sink is intended to carry the nitrate bath. I prefer this position for the nitrate bath, because it is so easy to examine the film when the bath is placed between yourself and the light. Care must however be taken that no splashes of developer, or dirty water, fall into the bath.

A shelf should be fixed close to the sink, on which to put the bottles of solution required in the manipulation. The rest of the room may be fitted up as its shape and size may suggest. I think it however a good plan to make the dark room a mere closet, cut off from a larger room by a suitable partition. The outer room may then have a fireplace in it, and be provided with suitable shelves, drawers, &c., for the various articles which are sure to accumulate, and which I will not alarm the reader by enumerating. He will find soon enough that Photography is a somewhat expensive pursuit, and that METHOD in his work and appointments will save him many pounds annually.

The dark room should be kept as clean as possible. There should be no cobwebs on the walls, or dust flying about. As for the floor, it is not in the power of man to keep that free from stains, so it need not be attempted.

APPARATUS.

I shall not devote a separate chapter to the Apparatus, because that can be better described by the optician who sells it; but a few remarks may not be out of place.

The vessel which contains the nitrate bath may be made either of glass, or gutta percha, but porcelain is objectionable, because nitrate of silver acts on, and cracks the glaze. I have never found any ill effects from keeping the nitrate bath perpetually in a vessel of gutta percha. But there is an impure kind of gutta percha adulterated with the gums of other trees, and with plaster of paris, which would no doubt react on the nitrate bath. Gutta percha vessels used in photography should be made of genuine gutta-percha.

A very simple plate-holder may be made by cutting three flat pieces of India rubber, each about an inch and half square, and half an inch thick, and sticking them together by heat. The flat outside piece when rendered slightly sticky by holding it before the fire will adhere to the under side of the plate, and hold it with just the proper amount of force. But I prefer taking the plate by one corner between the finger and thumb.

In order to save the hands from being stained, it is a good plan to wear the India rubber finger caps used by doctors, when dissecting; or better still, India rubber gloves, sold for the same purpose.

The Lens should have its chemical and visual foci coincident. Excellent pictures may no doubt be taken with lenses which are not achromatic, but they give a good deal of extra trouble to those who do not understand them.

Improvements may be made in the mounting of lenses. A stop should always be placed midway between the double lenses of a portrait combination, not for the purpose of cutting off any of the outer rays of the pencils, but in order to throw a shadow on the inside of the tube, and so prevent much reflected light from entering the camera and fogging the picture. The brass work should not be blackened with chloride of platinum, but with the old lamp black mixture, because the former method merely changes the colour, without destroying the polish of the metal. Portrait lenses should be screened by a dark funnel projecting in front of them, in order to cut off diffused light. Opticians are much to blame for not attending to all these points, which are of the utmost practical importance.

In purchasing a portrait lens, the reader should choose a large lens with a long focus, in preference to a small lens with a short focus. A lens of long focus will take a small picture quite as sharp as one of short focus, but the converse is not true; while the distance at which a lens of long focus is placed from the sitter enables the operator to get a flatter field, and avoid the distortion of the near and side objects, which is inevitable when a lens of short focus is employed. Lenses of long focus are rather slower than those of short focus, because their aperture is not generally made to increase in proportion to their focal length ; but this process is so extremely sensitive, compared with the Daguerreotype and Negative processes, that a little extra time of exposure hardly matters. The only drawback in using a lens of long focus occurs when the atmosphere is full of smoke, as often happens in large towns. In such cases the nearer the camera is brought to the sitter the better, and then a lens of short focus has its advantage in preventing fogging.

When a stop is used with a portrait lens, it may either be placed immediately before the front glass, or midway between the two double lenses. In the latter case it should have a smaller aperture than in the former, in order to produce an equivalent effect. I prefer the latter method, although mere convenience generally suggests the former.

A stereoscopic camera with double lenses, will sometimes be useful, as both pictures can then be taken at once, on the same plate. The circumstance of the axes of the lenses being parallel, and not converging to a point, does not introduce any practical objection. The only objection to the Stereoscopic Camera with two lenses is, that the stations are in general too close together to give sufficient stereoscopic effect. From four to eight inches are the best distances between the stations, when two cameras are employed. The duplicate pictures taken on one plate must not be separated if the film side of the glass has been presented to the lens. The portraits are however in this case reversed. When it is required to take non-reversed stereoscopic portraits on one plate, a non-reversing slide must be employed, and the pictures must be separated and transposed. In viewing stereoscopic pictures in the stereoscope, the picture taken from the right-hand station must be viewed by the right eye, and that from the left-hand station by the left eye; otherwise a pseudo-scopic effect is produced. The above statements have been very carefully considered, and are strictly correct.

A focusing glass is very useful to magnify the image on the ground glass, and enable the operator to get it in better focus.

A ground glass and slide for non-reversed portraits is a very useful addition to the camera. It is contrived thus:—

The coated plate is put in the slide so that the back may be next the lens, and not the coated side. The film is then protected by covering it with a glass plate, having a little triangular bit of glass cemented to each corner. The back of the slide when shut presses on this outer plate, instead of on the back of the coated plate in the usual way. The picture is then taken *through* the glass, and when black varnished on the back in the usual way, the portrait is seen non-reversed.

CHAPTER IV.

MANIPULATION OF THE PROCESS.

The Positive Collodion Process involves, as I have before stated, seven distinct operations, which are enumerated at Pages 24 and 25.

These operations I will now describe in the order in which they must be performed.

1st. Operation.—To CLEAN THE GLASS PLATE.

A few words first about the proper kind of glass to employ.

I recommend the best patent plate glass, for the following reason,—the surface has been carefully ground and polished. Now, smoothness of surface is a very important point in the present process, because roughness is found to occasion the precipitation of the silver under the action of the developer, even where light may not have acted. It is probable that light acts on a sensitive surface in two ways. It first crystallizes and roughens the iodide of silver in the film, and then deoxidises the free nitrate of silver immediately in contact with the roughened iodide. So that a rough surface to work upon may resemble to some extent iodide of silver that has been roughened by light, and in this way produce fogging. At any rate, it is a well known fact that common window glass, however perfectly cleaned, will frequently give a foggy picture, when plate glass does not. It also sometimes happens that one side of a piece of common glass being better polished than the other, gives the best picture.

It is advisable, therefore, to employ the best plate glass, which, from the less frequent occurrence of failures, will be found the most economical in the end. As a rule, I should say, avoid little questionable economies in Photography, and procure the best materials and apparatus. This is certainly a saving in the long run.

Black, or purple glass, is used by some operators, in order to avoid the necessity of applying black varnish to the back of the plate. Messrs. Forrest and Bromley, of Liverpool, are about to manufacture purple plate glass for this process, and I am sure it will be found a very useful article. The tone of positives taken on purple glass is very good, and the little difficulties which occur in the manipulation are soon overcome. The great objection to black varnish is its liability to crack.

Messrs. Kloen & Jones, of Birmingham, have recently patented a variety of tablets for Positive Collodion Photographs, which are intended to supersede glass for certain purposes. I possess, unfortunately, no information on this subject, of a satisfactory kind; and I should fear that pictures taken on these tablets, would be liable to fog, for reasons that have been stated. Experiment, however, must decide the point. I have seen positives taken on Talc, but none that I considered *quite* satisfactory. The slightest veil of fog over the blacks deprives a collodion positive, in my opinion, of one of its principal charms, viz., the transparency of the shadows.

The plate has now to be cleaned ;—

If the imperceptible roughness on a piece of common glass can occasion fog on the picture, it will readily be believed that a dirty plate may do so; and I need not dwell on the importance of rendering the plate chemically clean. This is very easily done. If the reader will observe the following directions, he will save himself a great deal of unnecessary trouble, and will never be annoyed by dirty glasses :—

Assuming that we have a dirty plate to deal with, or one of which we do not know the antecedents ;—first wash and rub it as clean as you can, in common water. Then take a wide-mouthed 4 oz. bottle. Half fill it with common Nitric Acid, and fill up with water. This dilute Nitric Acid is to be rubbed on the plate with a mop, made as follows :— Procure a thin glass rod, a foot long, and bend it in the middle, over a spirit lamp, until the ends come together, the two sides being nearly parallel. Then twist up a rope of cotton wool, and wind it in and out, round and between the glass rods, so as to form a mop with a glass handle. Secure it with a piece of cotton thread tied round the wool. Dip the mop in the Nitric Acid, and rub the plate all

D

over with it. Then wash *well* under a tap, and dry the plate, either by rubbing it with a clean cloth kept for the purpose, or by shaking it among boxwood dust; a couple of quarts of which may be kept in a cigar box. Next, polish the plate with a clean dry cambric rag, (not with silk, because the fine grain of silk would scratch the glass; nor with wash leather, because this might contain impurities).

The plate is now clean and ready for the next operation.

The treatment with Nitric Acid is not necessary every time the plate is used; it is only necessary with a plate that may be dirty. Washing with plain water is enough when you treat your glasses properly, and do not allow them to contract greasy stains and chemical impurities. Should a picture be unsuccessful, hold it at once under the tap, and rub off the film; then put it in a pan of water, to be cleaned at your convenience. Do not let it get dry; that is the great point to be avoided. By never letting the glass get dry, you will avoid the necessity for the Nitric Acid treatment. The Cyanide of Potassium, with which the pictures are fixed, is nearly as good a detergent as Nitric Acid, so that the plate has been really cleaned by the fixing solution, and will not require to be cleaned again, if you keep it under water, and do not let it dry spontaneously.

The varnish may be removed from an old plate by allowing it to remain for a few hours in a mixture of cinders and water.

. Never clean your glasses with tripoli, or a solution of soda, or ammonia, as some writers have recommended. A grit in the tripoli might scratch the glass all over. Its fine polish is also destroyed by rubbing with tripoli, and this is one cause of foggy pictures. Alkaline solutions do not remove grease unless they are boiling hot. They merely loosen and spread it over the plate. A few drops of Ether remove grease better than an alkali, because Ether combines readily with oils and fats, at an ordinary temperature.

Dirty cloths should not be washed in water containing soap. Boiling water alone should be used, after which they should be well rinsed.

2nd. Operation.—To APPLY THE IODIZED COLLODION.

First, wipe the neck of the bottle, in order to remove any little dry bits of Collodion, which might be transferred to the plate. Then, hold the plate horizontally, by one corner, between the finger and thumb of the left hand; blow off any dust that may have settled on it, and pour on the centre of it a circular patch of collodion, rather more than sufficient to cover it. Then, tilt the plate, so as to let the collodion run towards the thumb; next, not allowing it to touch the thumb, but leaving that corner dry, tilt it so as to let it run towards the other corners. As soon as the plate is covered, hold it vertically over the bottle, with the lower corner resting on it, and let the surplus collodion run into the bottle. Then rock the plate backwards and forwards in its own plane, half a dozen times, in order to prevent the formation of lines in the collodion ; then, place it on the dipper.

The surplus collodion should be allowed to drain from the corner which is diagonally opposite to that by which the plate is held.   This I think better than pouring it from the corner next the thumb, because that sometimes occasions the formation of a thick belt of collodion, along two edges of the plate.

3rd Operation.—To SENSITIZE THE FILM.

As soon as the surplus Collodion is poured off, the film begins to set, that is to say—the fluid becomes a jelly, in consequence of the evaporation of the Ether, and this jelly would in a few minutes harden into a skin. You may observe the line of setting advance across the plate. As soon as it has reached the lower corner, immerse the plate in the nitrate bath, quickly, and without hesitation, or lines would be formed across it.   You must also wash the plate crossways, beneath the fluid, in order to prevent the formation of lines in the direction of the dip.

This done, leave the plate in the bath, (where it may remain several minutes), while you arrange the sitter, and get the picture on the ground glass into good focus. The plate should remain at least two minutes in the bath, and it does not matter how much longer, when the bath contains a sufficient quantity of Iodide of Silver to prevent it from attacking the iodide in the film.

It is a good plan to keep the nitrate bath covered with a piece of gutta percha, attached to the dipper.

4th Operation.—To Expose in the Camera.

No picture can be considered a successful one, that is deficient in the details of the shadows. You must therefore expose for the shadows, not for the lights. By shadows, I do not mean those dark and impenetrable recesses which are in nature nearly devoid of light (such as creases in the dress), these should be preserved as absolute blacks in the picture, and you will find them represented by rich dark touches in fine works of art ; by shadows, I mean those parts which are not illuminated directly by the principal light, and which receive a modified or subdued light by reflexion from other objects. The exposure must be timed with respect to these half-shadows (as they are sometimes called), and without any reference to the lights, which must be left to take care of themselves.

Now see what follows inevitably from this rule. The amount of light in the half shadows, does not so much depend on the principal source of light, as on the reflecting power of the objects that happen to be placed near the sitter. The exposure could not therefore be reduced by a single second, were the sitter placed in full sunshine, *unless more light were reflected from adjacent objects on the parts in shadow.*

In the exposure, we have therefore nothing to do either with the high lights or the impenetrable shadows, but our whole attention must be given to the half shadows. Natural darkness will be represented in the finished picture by blacks (if the chemicals do not fog), and high lights by whites, if the exposure has not been pushed to such an extent as to solarize them, and thus render them grey and sombre.

We must therefore expose for the half shadows, and yet not over-expose for the lights. This can only be managed by diminishing the contrasts by the proper use of white screens as reflectors, as I have already described; and these should not be placed so as to interfere with the " tangential lines of shade." (See page 15). .

If these points are attended to, a process must be bad indeed which does not give soft and beautifully graduated pictures.

The artist must make a study of " light and shade." He must devote weeks and months, if need be, to this branch of his profession; and having once mastered it, he will soon find himself among those who stand at the top of the tree: for the mechanical part of photography is comparatively easy.

When all is ready to take the picture, lift the plate out of the bath. You will see it covered with lines, like those produced by water running from a greasy surface. These are caused by the ether which adheres to the film. They must be removed by raising the plate out of and lowering it into the bath seven or eight times, until the ether has been completely washed off. Then wipe the back of the plate thoroughly with blotting paper, and place it carefully in the slide, which should be clean and free from dust.

Carry the slide quickly to the camera, taking care always to hold it in an upright position, with the bottom of the plate downwards.

Look once more on the ground glass to see that all is right; then put the cap on the lens. Next, remove the ground glass and insert the slide in its place. The ground glass should be put out of harm's way, on a shelf, which you must yourself add to the camera stand, for opticians never attend to this matter. Then raise the shutter gently, in order to avoid dislodging any dust, and throw the black focusing cloth over the top and back of the camera.

All is now ready for the exposure.

Request the sitter to remain perfectly still for a few seconds, and then remove the cap from the lens. Count the number of seconds required for the exposure by a watch, which you hold in the left hand; or better still, by means of a pendulum, 40 inches long, suspended to the wall, and which has previously been set oscillating. Each oscillation, whether through a large or small angle, will occupy exactly one second of time.

Replace the cap on the lens, shut the slide and run quickly with it to the dark room.

The exposure required for a Positive is generally about half that which would be necessary for a Negative, or for a Daguerreotype plate.   It varies from two to twenty seconds, according to the light, lens, &c.   This is sufficiently rapid for all ordinary practical work.   The Positive Collodion process is the most sensitive at present known.

You may compare the rapidity of different portrait lenses very approximately, by the following rule :—

Measure the diameter of the front lens (or the front stop), in eighths of an inch, and also the distance of the ground glass from the middle point between the front and back lenses of the combination, in eighths of an inch. (The focal length, measured from the back lens, gives a very erroneous idea of the intensity of a portrait combination.)

Put the first of these quantities in the numerator, and the last in the denomination of a fraction. This fraction squared will then represent the intensity of the lens; and by means of it the relative intensities of different lenses may be compared.

A small trap door, or a flap of dark cloth, must be left in the side of the dark cone which projects beyond the lens, to enable you to turn the focusing screw.

If you find it awkward to take off and replace the cap to the lens, you may do without the cap, by simply allowing the black focusing cloth to hang over the front of the dark cone.

The exposure is of course a matter on which much depends. You must not push the development, as in the Negative process. There is a point at which you *must* stop, or you bury the finer shades of the lights. If you under-expose, the picture will present a few brilliant whites on a black ground, and no half-tones. If you over-expose, the picture will look flat and deficient in contrasts, besides being of a bad colour in the higher lights.

Never attempt to take pictures in a bad light. After working successfully all day, you will sometimes find that towards evening the pictures begin to fog. Then leave off. The peculiarity of the light is an enemy with which you cannot contend. On the morrow all will go well again. It is not that the lengthened exposure alone produces fogging, but some peculiarity in the light. When the light is good, you may use any diaphragm, and give the corresponding exposure, but when the light is of a certain character you will fail in getting a good picture. On this subject I will not venture to theorize. I merely mention a singular fact, which I believe all photographers must have observed when practising the Positive Collodion Process.

I must not omit to mention a circumstance which should be observed when focusing the sitter. The camera should be rather higher than the face, and made to point downwards at it. By employing this legitimate artifice, the lower features are foreshortened, and more height is given to the forehead. But this is not all. You will find that, owing to the plane of the picture not being vertical, all vertical lines are made to converge towards a point beneath the ground, and that the upper part of every object is ex-aggerated in width. You therefore, by this arrangement, increase the apparent breadth as well as height of the forehead.

5th Operation.—To DEVELOP THE PICTURE.

The sooner the picture is developed after being removed from the bath, the better. You must not wait so long as is sometimes allowable in the Negative process. Three or four minutes are a limit which you had better not exceed, between the removal of the plate from the bath, and pouring on the developer.

The development of a Glass Positive is unlike that of any other photograph. It is an exceedingly *smart* operation, and must be done almost at a blow. Pour sufficient developer into a glass measure to cover the plate abundantly with fluid, and then pour it on the plate, and by tilting and shaking, make it run all over *at once*. In a few seconds the picture is developed. As soon as you see the outline of any dark part tolerably defined, pour off the developer and wash the plate with water. Unless the picture comes out quickly it is sure to be worthless. The development is therefore a critical operation, and requires practice.

The developer runs very readily over the film, but you must use enough of it.

The developed picture has but little opacity. There is but little precipitate, the merest imaginable film through which light passes easily ; but this film of metal, thin as it is, produces an opaque white when seen by *reflected* light.

There is a little difficulty in developing on purple glass, because you cannot see so well what you are about, or view the picture by transparency. A little more light is required in the dark room, when purple glass is used.

You must not pour the developer from the plate to the measure, and back again, as in developing a negative. Nor must the same developer be used twice. Remember that the great enemy of this process is FOG on the plate, (that is, —a light veil which obscures the blacks).

6th Operation.—To FIX THE PICTURE.

As soon as the picture has been developed, wash it well under the tap, and pour on it the fixing solution. Then let daylight into the dark room, by drawing the sliding panel of the window, and watch the gradual disappearance of the yellow iodide of silver from the film. When it has all gone, wash well under the tap, in order to remove the Cyanide of Potassium. Leave none in, or it will destroy the picture· Then dry the plate before the fire, or over gas. The picture gets much whiter by drying. It may now be examined by holding it against a black sleeve, or by placing a piece of black oilcloth or black japanned tin behind it.

7th Operation.—To VARNISH THE PICTURE.

Apply the varnish in the same manner as the Collodion. First, varnish the film with the Transparent Varnish; and when dry apply the Black Varnish to the other side of the glass. Never black-varnish the film. This injures the colour of the lights; and should the varnish crack, the picture will be destroyed.

As soon as the black varnish is dry, paste a piece of paper over it, and put the picture at once into the frame which is to receive it.

I prefer a plain gold mat next the picture. The glass in front of it, should be of the very best quality, and absolutely colorless. Examine it edgeways, and if it looks at all green at the edge, reject it. Never exhibit any kind of photograph behind a green glass. But above all things, never put a glass positive into any kind of frame having a white border. The whites of a positive, however fine they may be, look dull and metallic, when contrasted with white paper. A Collodion Positive should be viewed in a strong light, in order to be seen to the best advantage.

The mode of colouring the picture will be given in the next chapter. Before concluding the present, I may however add a few words on the subject of transferring the picture from the glass plate to a sheet of paper, or other substance.

On referring to the advertisements at the end of this Treatise, the reader will find that a process of transferring Collodion Positives from glass to paper, has been patented by Mr. A. Rollason, of Birmingham. Another method of transferring is also advertised by Messrs. Butterfield and Co., of York, who supply the black varnish required in bottles, with directions for use. The method is perfectly successful.

I have succeeded in transferring collodion films from the glass to gelatinised paper, by a very simple plan, which I will describe ; but the film should be made with the sample of Gun-Cotton, No. 5, dissolved in Ether, S.G. .750, six parts, Alcohol, S.G. .820, two parts. This collodion gives a film rather harder, and more like a piece of skin, than that which I have described as most suitable for yielding a fine positive.

Proceed thus :—Having washed off the fixing solution, and while the film is still wet, remove with a penknife, about an eighth of an inch of film all down each side of the plate. Then lay the plate horizontally on the table, and apply to the film a piece of thick wet blotting paper, leaving one end of the film exposed. Turn this end neatly over the blotting paper, with the penknife, and then, commencing with this end, lift the blotting paper carefully off the plate. The collodion film will come off with it. Next, having previously gelatinised a piece of black glazed paper, or other black material, and allowed it to dry, apply the blotting paper, film side to it. Press them into contact. The film will then adhere to the gelatinised paper, and the blotting paper will come off clean. Allow the transferred picture to dry spontaneously.

Collodion negatives may be transferred in this way from the glass plate to a sheet of gelatine or gelatinised waxed paper ; but unfortunately the hard films, which are the most easily transferred, are not those which give the best pictures.

CHAPTER V.

ON THE MODE OF COLOURING COLLODION POSITIVES WITH DRY COLOURS.

The dry colours used in colouring Collodion Positives or Daguerreotypes, are sold in small glass bottles, corked, (not stoppered); and the colours are applied by means of small fine-pointed sable-brushes. Twenty or thirty different colours have been prepared, and from these the artist may make his selection according to his taste.

The colours are generally put on after the picture has been varnished, but the better plan is,—first, to apply to the film, while still wet with the last washing water, a coating of gelatine, and to colour on that; varnishing afterwards; and a second time retouching the picture, if necessary, on the varnish.

The gelatine solution should be made in the proportion of two grains of gelatine to one ounce of water, and applied tepid. When dry, the colours may be put on.

Only a very small quantity of colour is required. Some operators empty a little out of the bottle on a piece of card, but a better plan is to use that which adheres to the under side of the cork, after inverting the bottle, and so to make the cork your pallette. Apply it with the point of the brush by means of a continued circular motion.

With respect to the proper colours to employ; I need not tell the artist, that he is not to use green for the hair, nor blue for the cheeks, nor red for the eyes. He must use the colours which appear to him to be most appropriate. No rules can be laid down; and the only suggestions that I can offer are those which relate to the broad principles of colouring. As a rule then, let him avoid pure crude colours. These are rarely found in nature; and in the works of fine colourists they are only introduced in occasional touches, in order to give value by contrast to the other tints. If the reader will take the trouble to paint half-a-dozen pieces of card, with pure unmingled blues, reds, and yellows, and take them with him to the National Gallery, or Marlborough House (I will not say the Royal Academy), and compare them with the blues, reds, and yellows, in the pictures of Etty, Titian, Rubens, and other great colourists, he will find that the works of these masters are painted in a comparatively low tone of colour, with the exception of the occasional touches of pure bright colour which give value to the other tints. Or, if he will go out of doors, and compare his painted cards with the colours of natural objects, by holding one of them at arms length, between his eye and the object with which it is to be compared, he will discover that nature rarely indulges in such freaks of colour as to afford him a match to his crude pigments. As a rule, therefore, the colours to be employed should be subdued by mixture, and never composed of less than three pure tints ; the latter being only used occasionally as a means of heightening the effect of the rest.

Some years ago, I had the good fortune to know Mr. Etty and I used to go and see his pictures, in his studio in Buckingham-street, before they were sent to the Royal Academy for exhibition. On these occasions I used to attempt to analyse his mode of colouring. I remember being much struck with his " Judgement of Paris," as a superb example of colour. The " Juno " in particular, accompanied by her peacock, and about to drive off disdainfully in a golden chariot was a *chef-d'œuvre* of colour. But here I remarked that there were no crude tints, except perhaps in the highest lights.

The other day I went over the collection of Mr. Sheepshanks, at Knightsbridge, and had occasion to make the same remark with respect to the three fine Turners which hang opposite the windows in his drawing room. Here again there was but little crude colour. Nothing but subdued tints, and now and then a bright touch introduced just to enhance their value by contrast. Yet these pictures seem all " light and air."

E

In one of Sir Joshua Reynolds's lectures he mentions that once putting his card against the sun of a painting by Claude, he was amazed at its low tone of colour. Could he have cut out that sun and mounted it on his card he says it would have appeared, when out of the picture, a dirty yellow patch; and yet, in its place, when contrasted with the other tints, it became a glowing source of light.

I say, therefore, avoid crude colours; or only use them sparingly, as a means of heightening the effect of the other sober tints.

But I do not at all approve of the practice of tinting Collodion Positives. It appears to me to be opposed to sound principles of taste, for this reason,—that in tinting a collodion positive, or daguerreotype, you are only allowed to tint the lights, and must not meddle with the shadows. The picture cannot therefore be anything but a lame production. No true artist would think of painting a picture on such terms. The great charm of colour lies in the harmonious blending of lights and shadows, and the latter are capable of exhibiting quite as much variety and beauty of tint as the lights. A tinted positive can never therefore aspire to be a work of art. It can be, at the best, but a bungling production, only fit to amuse a childish and uneducated taste. A *bond fide* photograph has its peculiar merits; but once touched by the artist, fettered as he is in the present instance, it can become neither a work of art, nor a truthful representation of anything natural or possible.

I object therefore, on principle, to the application of dry colours to photographic portraits of this class. The same objections do not, however, apply to positives on paper. Here the shadows may be retouched as well as the lights, and the photograph may legitimately become the ground of a water colour drawing, possessing all the qualities of a fine work of art. Photography is, in this department of portraiture, a boon to the portrait painter, and a great step in his art.

It has been proposed to tint paper positives with dry colours; but how, I ask, are the shadows to be treated in such a process? How is their transparency to be preserved? Dry or opaque colours may properly enough be used in the lights, if the artist does not object to painting over the photograph, but wet transparent colours can alone be used in the shadows. I caution the reader, therefore, against falling into an error on this point.

I have said nothing of the use of gold and silver shells. Those who are pleased with tinted cheeks, ribbands, ties, &c., may certainly be indulged with gold and silver finery I see nothing incongruous in it.

CHAPTER VIII.

THEORY OF THE PROCESS.

I regret to say that our knowledge of the Theory of this Process is very imperfect; but I will endeavour to state clearly the little that is known, and to offer some speculations on what is hypothetical.

The collodion is the mere vehicle in which the chemical reactions take place. It appears to remain nearly, if not absolutely, inert during the operations, and its office is simply mechanical, viz., to retain the chemicals within its pores, or on its surface, and thus fasten the picture to the glass. The film of pyroxyline undergoes little or no change during the operations. It is as explosive and as soluble in ether, after the picture has been taken on it, as it was when first made.

The film of iodized collodion that is spread on the glass plate contains throughout its entire substance the alkaline iodide. When immersed, in its gelatinous state, in the nitrate bath, the Nitrate of Silver penetrates the film completely and decomposes every atom of Iodide of Ammonium, forming by a double decomposition, Iodide of Silver and Nitrate of Ammonia. Some of the latter salt is transferred to the bath, but the larger portion of it remains in the film. The free Iodine which gives the red tint to the Iodized Collodion forms with the Nitrate of Silver, Iodide of Silver, and Iodate of Silver. The latter salt I have proved to exert no influence either for good or harm in the subsequent operations; and the same may be said of the Nitrate of Ammonia. In addition to the Iodide of Silver a portion of free Nitrate of Silver remains in the film. Iodide of Silver is a yellow salt, and this gives to the film its peculiar colour.

The sensitive film contains therefore principally Iodide of Silver and free Nitrate of Silver, which salts pervade its entire substance.

The presence of free Nitrate of Silver is absolutely necessary in order to obtain an impression; and the highest condition of sensitiveness is probably that in which every atom of Iodide of Silver has an atom of Nitrate of Silver in juxta-position with it. Either more or less free nitrate than this appears to diminish the sensitiveness of the film.

When the sensitive surface is exposed to light, a change of some sort, either molecular or electrical, is produced in the Iodide of Silver, which however is not decomposed, but probably crystallized. When this state of things is produced,

the atom of Nitrate of Silver in contact with the crystallised
or altered Iodide, is loosened in the affinities which bind
together the Nitric Acid and the Oxide of Silver, and these
either separate, or become ready to separate, in presence of a
further disturbing force such as the developer.

In consequence of the transparency of the film, its moist
state, and its thorough saturation so to speak with the
sensitive chemicals, no obstacles are presented to the action
of light. Particles are free to move, affinities are free to
act, the light penetrates everywhere, and the whole mass of
sensitive matter under its influence is acted on readily.
Hence the extraordinary sensitiveness of the moist Collodion
process when compared with dry Albumen, or Paper,
where the same mechanical conditions of the medium do
not exist.

The developer is a de-oxydizing agent. It demands
Oxygen of the Nitrate of Silver, and the salts of the Prot-
Oxide of Iron (the proto-sulphate and proto-nitrate) by
receiving this Oxygen become converted into salts of the
Per-Oxide of Iron (the per-sulphate and per-nitrate). The
Oxide of Silver, through the loss of its oxygen, becomes
converted into metallic silver; Nitric Acid is liberated ;
but the Iodide of Silver still remains unchanged.

The Nitric Acid in the bath and developer prevents those
parts of the picture that have not been acted on by light
from being decomposed by the developer. It is probable

that in those parts the developer becomes oxydised at the expense of the Nitric Acid instead of the Nitrate of Silver, which there remains unchanged.

The image is therefore formed by the precipitation of metallic silver. This silver is obtained from two sources. First, the atom of Nitrate which was in contact with the altered atom of Iodide of Silver is decomposed, and metallic silver reduced ; and, secondly, the excess of Nitrate in the film is reduced, and a further precipitation of silver takes place, not indiscriminately over the whole plate, but only on the atoms that have been previously reduced. Thus, as the development goes on, metallic silver is heaped together on the same parts, in masses which form the lights of the picture.

The colour of these masses, when viewed by reflected light, depends, I imagine, on the molecular arrangement of the layer of atoms that are last precipitated, and is brown, or grey, or white, or of metallic lustre, according to the rapidity with which the precipitation takes place. Strong, rapid developers, such as Pyrogallic Acid, or Proto-Sulphate of Iron, give a brown, bad colour to the lights ; and a slow developer, such as Proto-Nitrate of Iron, gives them a metallic crystalline appearance. Both are bad, but the happy mean is obtained by combining the rapid proto-sulphate with the slow proto-nitrate in the proportions which I have given ; and thus a beautiful dead white precipitate is produced.

Alcohol is added to the developer, to enable it to flow more readily over the film.

Cyanide of Potassium fixes the picture,—that is to say,—removes the redundant chemicals which would be further acted on by light, by forming with the Iodide of Silver a double salt, viz :—a double Cyanide of Silver and Potassium, together with Iodide of Potassium.

The final washing leaves nothing but metallic silver in the film.

I have endeavoured to show in *Phot. Notes*, No. 19, that this process resembles in some important points the Electrotype, and my remarks have been followed in No. 21, by an interesting letter signed " ALPHA," in which fresh facts are adduced in favour of this hypothesis, and new analogies between the two processes pointed out.

The gradual darkening of the Iodized Collodion by keeping, which is due to the liberation of free Iodine, is a matter which has puzzled chemists considerably. I think it most probably occasioned by the liberation of Nitrous Acid from the Pyroxyline ; an atom of Oxygen would thus be left in the Pyroxyline, instead of the Peroxide of Nitrogen ; which might happen to a substitution compound like Pyroxyline, without altering its character. The liberated Nitrous Acid would then decompose the Iodide of Ammonium and form Hypo-nitrite of Ammonia, the Iodine being liberated. This effect does not occur to the same extent with Iodide of Cadmium because that metal is not so easily oxydized and acted upon by the acid, and its affinity for iodine is strong.

CONCLUDING REMARKS.

I have said nothing of the merits of this process as compared with its rival, the Daguerreotype. Both are equally simple and certain in the hands of the experienced operator, and each has its advantages. In point of microscopic definition and exquisite gradation of shade, there is no process which, in my opinion, can be compared with that of Daguerre, and for scientific purposes no other should be employed. But for portraiture the shimmer of the plate is generally considered so serious a drawback that the Daguerreotype has now become almost obsolete. For my own part I do not participate in this feeling, and I predict that sooner or later there will be a reaction in favour of the metal plate. But in the meantime we must make the most we can of the present process, and not attempt to argue with people who will not be convinced. A good glass Positive is much bolder in effect than a Daguerreotype, and is free from the objection of the metallic shimmer. When the whites are good, the picture free from fog, and the half-tones properly brought out, a glass positive becomes a highly artistic production, and is entitled to rank with any other kind of photograph in this respect. As regards permanence, we know that metallic silver is readily tarnished by sulphuretted hydrogen, but, protected from this deleterious gas, the Collodion Positive is no doubt as permanent as any other description of photograph, if not more so.

In point of definition, no printed positive on paper or glass can compare with one that is taken by a direct process.

Such are the merits of the process described in these pages, and I may add one more, viz., its economy. It is a cheap process, and on that account fit for those professional portraitists who work for a small remuneration, and whose labours have the good effect of placing a photographic portrait within the reach of the humbler classes.

And who would not wish the poor man to participate in that great domestic luxury—a photographic portrait of those near and dear to him? Photography, as applied to portraiture, is one of the greatest blessings of the age in which we live, and a real social good. Few are so desolate as to be exempt from the moral obligation now imposed on them, of obtaining a photographic portrait of those who may be bound to them by intimate ties of blood or friendship. I say a " moral obligation," and I am not using too strong an expression. Who knows what a day may bring forth, or the inestimable value that any one of the chances of life may suddenly confer on a photographic portrait (however bad), or the remorse which may follow the neglect of the duty which I am now suggesting, when it is too late to fulfil it?

I am aware of the many imperfections of this hastily written treatise, and anxious to remedy them. I beg therefore of the reader, should he encounter any difficulty in carrying out my directions, to apply to me for further information, which I shall be happy at all times to give, either by private letter, or through the medium of " Photographic Notes."

ERRATUM.

Page 40, third paragraph. Instead of—" First, add together four ounces of powdered Asphaltum, and one ounce of common Benzole," read,—

" First, add together one ounce of powdered Asphaltum, and four ounces of common Benzole."